BEDTIME STORIES FOR KIDS

Wonderful Fairy Tales Will Lead your Children into a Magical World of Knights and Princesses, Developing Their Imagination and Values.

KATIE MILLER

Table of Contents

Introduction

Telling bedtime stories to young children can also foster a better attention span: learning to listen carefully, to pick up on verbal and physical cues, and to develop patience for the slow building of a well-told story are all key to healthy development in young children. Creating an interactive environment for the story is also crucial: asking questions and encouraging responses teaches children to engage deeply with the story, utilizing analytical skills and testing emotional reactions. This practice also encourages the child to take ownership of the storytelling process, giving them some space to test their thoughts and draw their conclusions.

Finally, the bedtime story is undeniably a powerful conduit for the passing on of certain values and beliefs: while not every bedtime story needs to have a "moral," many do and for very good reasons. These stories can help a parent to establish the parameters of appropriate behavior in children, as well as inculcate them with beliefs or ideas that are important to a particular worldview. They also serve to assist a child in the navigation of a grown-up world full of initially peculiar expectations ("why in the world should I eat with a fork or use a napkin?"; "what's the purpose of this please and thank you nonsense?"). Thus, bedtime stories can help to establish basic expectations and clarify certain boundaries.

1 - The Great and Noble King

A long time ago, in a very distant territory, lived a widowed king with his beloved children, Princes Rah, Reh, and Roh. The boys were triplets and were very much alike physically: all three had almost violet-blue eyes, whitish skin, shoulder-length wavy hair, and an exquisite natural elegance inherited from their mother. Since their birth they had received the same education and privileges, but the truth is that although at first glance they used to be confused, in terms of their way of being, they were completely different.

Rah was a slightly uptight, superficial, and the refined-tasting young man who cared a lot about his appearance. He liked nothing more than living surrounded by luxury and adorning himself with jewels; the bigger, the better! Reh, on the other hand, did not attach much significance to material belongings; he was the classic born joker who radiated joy at all hours and whose goal in life was to labor little and enjoy a lot. Roh, the third brother, was the shyest and calm; passionate about art and culture, he used to spend the afternoons writing poems, playing the harp, or reading old books in the palace's lavish library.

On their eighteenth birthday, the monarch wanted to give them a very special gift, and that is why, after a succulent family breakfast, he brought them together in the room where the most solemn acts and audiences were held. From his authority chair of gold and red velvet, he looked fortunately at the boys who, standing in front of him, were wondering why their father had summoned them at such an early hour.

"My children, today is a crucial day in your life. It seems like yesterday when you came into the world and look at each other now, and you are already grown men! Time flies by, doesn't it?"

Excitement broke his voice, and he had to pause a little before he could continue his speech.

"I have to confess that I have been thinking for months what to give you on this important occasion, and I sincerely hope that you like what I have arranged for you."

He picked up a small mother-of-pearl box that rested on the table beside him, and from inside, he took out three small leather bags tied with a golden thread.

"Come closer and get one each!"

The ancient king made the arrangement and kept talking.

"Each bag contains one hundred gold coins. I think that it is enough for you to go on a journey for a month! You are already grown-ups, so you have the freedom and autonomy to do what you want and spend the money as you please."

The boys looked at each other dumbfounded. One month to do what they want, how they want, and where they want, and on top of that with all expenses paid! Listening to the word 'gift,' they had imagined a gala cape or silk breeches, but this magnificent surprise was not at all.

"The only condition is that you leave the palace this noon, so go pack your luggage while the servants saddle up the horses. In thirty days, not one more, not one less, and exactly at this time, we will meet here, and you will tell me your experience. Okay?"

The three young men, still puzzled, thanked their father and gave their father a big hug. Then, floating in a cloud of happiness, they went to their rooms with their pockets full and their heads brimming with projects for the next four weeks. The clock struck twelve o'clock, and the princes left the place, decided to enjoy a unique and unforgettable month. Obviously, each one took the direction that he wanted according to his plans.

Rah decided to ride east because the richest and most influential noble families were concentrated there, and he believed that the time had come to meet them. Reh, like the good livelihood he was, went straight to the

South in search of sun and joy. He needed a party and knew where to find it! Unlike his brothers, Roh decided that it was best not to make strategies and travel the kingdom without a fixed path, without a precise destination to go to.

Day after day, weeks passed until finally, it was time to return and appear in the seat room to give an account to the king. Within a few minutes, the princes greeted their father, who received them with an affectionate hug.

"Welcome, my children. You cannot imagine how much I have missed you! This castle was so empty without you. What are you waiting for to tell me about your adventures? You have me on edge!"

Rah was excited and willing to be the first to tell his story. Looking at his father and brothers, he expanded,

"The truth is that I had a magnificent trip! It didn't take me more than a couple of days to get to the most prosperous city in the kingdom."

"Wow, that's great! And how did they receive you?"

"Wow, wonderfully! As soon as the aristocrats found out about me, they entertained me with parades, fireworks, and all kinds of festivities. Also, of course, when I stayed there, I stayed in elegant palaces, tasted exquisite delicacies, and was introduced to a beautiful and sophisticated duchess who stole my heart."

Rah stared into infinity, nostalgically recalling those moments so special to him. When he came to, he showed everyone his bag of coins.

"Look at my sack... it's still full! I have been asked to do everything, so of the hundred coins, I have only spent three. A month of luxury for the face! What is good?"

Rah's self-assurance made his father giggle.

"Ha ha ha! It is obvious that you have delighted, and I am very pleased for you."

Then the king saw another of his sons.

"And what about you, Reh, have you had as much fun as your brother?"

The nice boy was also mad with joy.

"Oh, yes, yes, even better! I can confirm without lying that it has been the best month of my life!"

"Don't tell me! We are eager to know your adventures."

"It is hard to recapitulate everything that I have experienced in a few words! But, I will only tell you that shortly after leaving, I found some wagons in which a company of many artists were traveling. They did not recognize me, so I told them that I was a cloth merchant going south, and they let me join the group. It was awesome! In each town they went to, they put on a show that left everyone astonished. There were tightrope walkers, clowns, and even fakirs!"

"Wow! That sounds good! It must have been a lot of fun!"

Reh was exalted, remembering his experiences.

"Yes! I would sit in the audience to watch it, but the best thing came later because once they collected the gear, we would go to dinner and party under the moonshine. Oh, what a carefree life that society has! If it weren't for the fact that I am the king's son, I assure you I would be a juggler."

Reh also stared blankly during, basking in his memories. Moments later, he added:

"By the way, they provided me couch and food in exchange for washing the dishes. I had so little expenses that I bring back almost all the coins I took!"

The father sighed, thinking that his son was hopeless.

"Oh, my dear Reh, when will you settle down? Look how you love to do indulgences! In any case, I am glad that this trip has been so enjoyable for you."

Finally, it was the third brother's turn.

"Well, you are left. Tell us how you have been..."

Roh didn't seem too satisfied.

"Well, I desired to perceive with my own eyes how the residents of our kingdom live. For a month, I toured all the farmhouses I could and talked to many agriculturalists about the things that concerned them the most, like the shortage of seeds and the lack of rain in recent years. I must say that everyone was very nice and shared what they had, even if it was little."

The king fixed his look on the young man and asked:

"It doesn't sound too funny, actually. My son, would you want to explain to me how all that has served you?"

Roh answered without hesitation,

"To see reality! To know what happens beyond the palace walls! Those of us who are here have everything, but out there, most of the population works from dawn to dusk under very harsh circumstances. Did you know that many do not have an old plow to facilitate their field tasks? And that the majority survive on bread and cheese because they have nothing else to put in their mouths?"

Despite the fact that what he was telling was very depressing, Roh did not fall apart and said the positive part of the trip.

"The virtuous thing is that I have taken note of all, and I came to a lot of concepts and ideas that we can carry out to progress the living circumstances of all those individuals! As for my money, I am sorry to say that I come with an empty bag because I distributed them to the neediest."

15

The king, very excited, got up and in a deep voice announced:

"When I decided to invite you to see the 'out there' for a month, I desired you to live an irreplaceable experience following the orders of your heart."

The surprised princes held their breath as their father grew more serious than usual.

"But I have to admit that it was also a trick to put you to the test. Look at me. I'm already an older man! I need to rest and spend my remaining years taking care of the plants in the garden, resting, and walking my animals. The time has come for this domain to have a new ruler to leader its destiny!"

The king sighed wearily.

"As you must know, the integrity and inheriting of the crown always fall on the eldest son, the heir, but in this case is impossible because, as you know, you were born on the same day. Therefore, I believe that my successor should be the one who most deserves it of the three."

He removed the sparkling emerald crown, placed it on the palm of his hands, and approached his children. The first words were for Rah.

"Dear Rah, you have become a man who achieves everything you set your mind to. You like to live well, and I praise it, but I hope that spending your days among lace and porcelain does not rot your honorable heart. Never forget to nurture a prodigious virtue: generosity, which will permit you to share part of how much you possess with those who have less. I wish you love and cheerfulness for your entire life."

Rah lowered his head, and the king walked a couple of steps until Reh was a few inches away.

"Dear Reh, you have turned out to be a man who knows how to enjoy everything that surrounds you. You want strong emotions, and I see that you will live with power until the end of your days. I just expect that so much enjoyment does not turn you into an unfilled being with nothing to offer to people. Try to make your life valuable, leave a significant legacy that will never be gone. I wish you love and cheerfulness for the rest of your life."

Finally, the king approached good Roh.

"Dear Roh, you have become a cultivated and empathetic man. You have taken the benefit of all these years to learn and train as best you can because you have perfectly understood what the responsibilities of a prince are. You are interested in the welfare of your people, and you are concerned with the neediest. My heart says to me that you are the selected one."

Then, to the amazement of Prince Rah and Prince Reh, he placed the crown on his head.

"From today on, you will be the king of this realm. Rule with reasonableness, and you will bring wealth, rule with goodness, and you will be treasured, rule with reason, and you will be valued for generations to come. I wish you love and cheerfulness for the rest of your life."

And so, for the first time, the best birthday gift served for a monarch to choose his successor. Apparently, it was a wise decision, perhaps the wisest of his life, because according to legend, Roh, the new king, fought to create a less unequal society, promoted great reforms, and entered history under the name of Roh the great and noble Kind.

In the end, empathy and love for others is a great gift that we all possess. We just have to awaken it within us and remember it.

2 - Num and the King

Many, many years ago, a jester named Num was invited to attend the birthday party of the King of Countraid. This Kingdom was so far from here that we would have to go around the planet three whole times to get there. Num was a pretty famous jester. After all, he always knew what to say to cheer people up because he was hilariously funny and always had entertaining stories to tell. He was just a genius.

When he was very young, Num's parents enrolled him in the jester school because they understood that he was a child prodigy. He learned to tell jokes even before he knew how to say 'mama' or 'papa,' to dance before knowing how to walk and sing before eating. Our friend Num graduated with honors and soon began to travel around the world to become the life of the party for many royal banquets, weddings, celebrations, national days, ceremonies, fifteen years, and birthdays of great Kings of all kinds of empires.

Num was invited to Countraid, the distant Kingdom, because its King, Lord Machareno III, wanted to enjoy his best jokes in celebration of his 50th birthday. He promised a colossal banquet, filled with all the dishes that Num loved: there were lobsters covered in chocolate with spicy cream and French fries; raspberry ice cream with pineapple jam syrup; gigantic split bananas with sweet little balls of tutti fruit; cookie meringue with strawberries and lemon; bacon pizzas with corn and heavy cream; and they even promised him a soup of crabs that would dance in the broth by itself.

Num didn't think much of it—the delicious meals that would await him there immediately convinced him. He took his suitcases and put in them all the toys that he would use for jokes, all the costumes he could wear to surprise the party guests, and all her magical tools. Num also had supernatural powers and wanted to put together the most spectacular show of magical lights, stars, and songs they had ever seen in that distant Kingdom. That is why Num, the Jester, was so well known—he put all his efforts into his work, to make others happy, to bring joy to bitter hearts.

"This is going to be a fun trip! Everyone at Countraid will be happy after I show them my fantastic show!" He said enthusiastically.

Then Num, the Jester, set out for Countraid, the distant and unknown realm. On the way, he crossed a great ocean with the magic boots that allowed him to float above the water; he crossed an immense forest where carnivorous plants were abundant in every corner. He made a snake barbecue on the top of a volcano because he liked the smoky flavor that the lava provided in the food until it finally reached its destination. But what he saw was not at all what he expected to find.

When he arrived at the town, he noticed that it was colored with the ugliest gray he had ever seen in his life. Num, the Jester, had visited many Kingdoms during his short existence and had seen many peculiar cities, but never a city so sad, so dull, and so gray!

"Who would ever think that coloring this place gray was a good idea? So many colors in the world and they come to choose gray!"

Then, Num looked at his clothes and realized that not only the town had been colored gray—he had lost all his colors!

"What kind of weird joke is this? Who was the funny guy who painted me this dirty color without my permission?"

Then Num, the Jester, took out his magic brush. All the villagers approached where our protagonist was. They wore sad looks and off as if they were robots in automatic mode. Num took his paintbrush, went Zim, Zam! and soon his clothes and his body had recovered their cheerful and fresh hues.

"That way, they will learn not to mess with a magical jester's wardrobe!" said Num.

At that moment, the locals began to clap and cry tears of joy. Num didn't understand why they did it.

"What's wrong with them? Have you never seen a colorful jester like me?"

"No, mister jester... We applauded because we had never seen colors like those before. Seeing so many together, we couldn't help but cry."

Num was very upset upon hearing those words.

"How can that be true? It is totally unfair that you have never seen colors! There has to be an explanation for this."

"All we know is that all the citizens of Countraid suffer the same, Mr. Num."

"Then, we are going to do something to change that situation!" Num blew magic strokes here and there, over sad men, bored animals, tiresome houses, and unpleasant streets. Soon, he filled all of that part of the town with beautiful colors.

"I can't believe it," said an old lady, "we finally got our colors back!" You are the most fantastic jester of all, Num! My skin had been painted gray for over 30 years..."

"30 years? And why did that change happen?" Num asked, curious.

"What happened was that Machareno III became the King of this beautiful Kingdom. Since he arrived, all the streets turned gray. Everyone became bored. All life became sad."

Num said goodbye to the locals who had managed to paint in colors and continued on his way to the royal court. "So Machareno III is responsible for this town having no colors? I'm going to ask that guy for explanations..." Num said, furious.

When Num got close enough to the magnificent Countraid Castle, a troop of royal soldiers came out to greet him, accompanied by trumpeters, drummers, flute players, and other musicians who played instruments with names so strange they didn't even know. Num, the Jester, was pleased for a few seconds, but then he remembered what the King had done to the inhabitants of his city.

"Although I am receiving beautiful music and with all the decorations that I deserve as your guest, there is something here that does not smell at all good," thought Num.

They filed forward until they reached the gates of the beautiful castle. When they were open, a huge bridge was unfolded so that Num the Jester and his company could cross the river. As he walked through the door, Num froze and closed his eyes—it was as if he had passed through a strange magic bubble. When he opened his eyes, Num realized that the castle interior was full of all the colors that have always existed throughout the world. The only thing missing was gray.

Num, the Jester, was led into the big dining room, where hundreds of guests sat waiting for the royal banquet to be finally served. King Machareno III was at the head of the table, and he rose to receive our dear friend.

"You finally arrived, Num! We wanted to meet you. You are the main work of my great 50th birthday, my friend.

I hope you are as good at doing shows as the rumors say!"

"Uh... yeah, I'm even better," Num, the Jester, told him. But I have a question to ask you, King Machareno III."

"Are you going to ask me questions and not even congratulate me on my big 50th birthday?" asked King Machareno III, in a mocking tone that irritated Num enormously.

"Ah, yes. Happy birthday, King!"

"What little emotion I feel in your voice, Num, the jester! It seems like you are upset with me..."

"Not that exactly, but I do need to ask you about."

"Enough, enough! All the matters that we should discuss will come after your show and the banquet. The guests have been waiting for you for a long time, and they must be quite hungry by now."

Num reluctantly agreed. He did not like King Machareno III.

Num caught the attention of all the guests in the big dining room. He took out of his hat a golden flower that shone as if the sun had come down to the earth and gave it to the fattest woman in the whole place, causing her to blush with emotion, then she began to do one of the most beautiful fun dances she had in her repertoire.

Although he initially thought the audience would be filled with cocky, insolent, arrogant, and vain characters, he found that they all seemed to be quite friendly. All except for King Machareno III, who badly treated his employees and he made rude and hurtful comments every time he opened his nasty monarch mouth.

Num, the Jester, told a joke about a parrot falling in love with a dolphin and everyone in the castle laughed aloud. Then, he made a show of lights that floated throughout the room, and that ended up transforming into an amazing giant chandelier. To finish his act, he took out his magic brush and said:

"Do you want to know what surprised me the most when I arrived in this Kingdom?"

"Yes!" they all responded. King Machareno III looked at him, suspicious of his plans."

"It was this!"

Num, the Jester, took his brush and went 'Zim, Zam!' throughout the room. The entire dining room lost its magnificent colors, and the guests showed their amazement when they perceived how the whole life had turned gray.

"This is surprising, Num," the guests were saying, "but it's too horrible! Could you please return the color to us?"

"I will when King Machareno III explains to me why all of Countraid is painted gray except for the interior of this castle!"

The guests looked at their King in great astonishment. Machareno III glared at Num, the jester.

"Dad, is that true? Do all our people suffer without colors?" asked the King's son.

"Yes, all of that is true!" exploded King Machareno III.

The entire royal family and guests began to make disapproving remarks at him. None of them agreed with taking the color out of their people. At that moment, Machareno III took out a magic wand from his tunic pocket, and made 'Piss, Pas!' And the whole room regained its lost color.

"I will tell the truth to all of you," King Machareno III was saying. Since I ascended the throne 30 years ago, I have stolen the colors from the people of Countraid to keep them for myself..."

"Why did you do that, dad? Are you crazy?" his son asked him.

"No, I'm not! You didn't even care if that happened until this fool" he pointed at Num the Jester. "Told you about it! They have lived all their lives in this castle, and they lack nothing. I wanted those colors for myself and our family exclusively! The villagers of our country do not deserve to have all this magic, all this light! You should not question me, I am your King, and I am always right!"

"Machareno III, you do not deserve to be a King," Num the jester told him with a serious tone that it would have scared the greatest of the giants.

"Oh yeah? Why?" Machareno III said, challenging him.

"A King must always put his people before himself. You don't deserve that crown, and you don't deserve to be the leader of your Kingdom."

"I'm going to make you apologize, Num, the Jester! Raise your wand. I challenge you to a duel!"

At that moment, the most astonishing, spectacular, and fabulous magical clash occurred in the tranquil Contraid Kingdom. The King fired explosive lights here and there, which Num the jester rejected with his wand and transformed them into simple soap bubbles. Num flicked his wrist, and suddenly all the lamps in the dining room went out. Machareno III fell to the ground and began to cry because he was terrified of the dark. Num shot him with his wand to disarm him and then lifted him into the air. Told him:

"Machareno III, for having stolen the colors and happiness of all your people out of simple selfishness, I will make you what you are!"

Num began to dance very quickly while waving her wand. Suddenly, a swift beam shot from its tip and shot towards King Machareno III, turning him into a chicken.

"Take what you deserve, bad King! That is my birthday present for you!"

At that instant, the light returned to the room. The royal family met and proposed that the Prince, Theodore II, to become the King.

"I am sorry for everything my father did to our people. Could you help us restore color throughout the Kingdom?" Asked the new King.

"Of course, my friend!"

The faraway Countraid Kingdom soon regained its color with the help of Num, the jester's magic brush. The new King promised that he would hold huge banquets inside the castle so that everyone in his town could enter to enjoy in union with the royal family.

"Num the Jester, what can we do to thank you for what you have done for our Kingdom?" Theodore II asked.

"It's simple! Prepare a banquet with all the delicious dishes that your father had promised me."

Num, the Jester, returned home happily, and from now on, everyone was happy and joyous in the distant Kingdom of Countraid.

3 - Caroline, the Fairy, and the Haunted Princess

Long ago, in a time so ancient, there were goblins stealing children to turn them into crickets and Princes fighting Dragons to save their loved ones. There was a big-hearted fairy named Caroline, and this is her story.

At that time, there were many fairies all over the planet. They were small beings that could be mistaken for children, with faces as pretty as a mother when smiles, with wings that allowed them to fly to the stars without fear of falling, and with amazing powers, they used to do good when necessary.

Every time a little girl came to this world and said her first word, a fairy was born, from the magic dust and the clouds cold breeze, to be her protector. In this sense, fairies lived to be a girl's companions, to keep them safe from any danger, to guide them on the right path, and to make them laugh when it's necessary. The goal of all fairies at birth was to meet their girls, but they could take a long time to meet.

"We are fairies, the strongest beings in the whole world! —The teacher Brume said during the class that dictated in the school for fairies— it does not matter if a Dragon comes, an ice-breathing dinosaur or a giant world-destroying monster! We must always be there, standing firm with our girls, to protect them from any possible danger!"

"We must always be there firmly with our girls to protect them from any danger!" repeated the little fairies.

When the magic moment arrived, all the fairies felt a supernatural call that told them that they should go to meet their girl. Then, they left the magical forest where all fairies were born and lived, and went to the outside world until they found the girls who were destined for them.

Caroline was a chubby fairy with a big heart, who, since she was a little fairy baby, waited to feel the call of her little girl soon. She had many fairy friends, such as Brittany, Bennifer, Lula, Monica, Veronique, and Rome, and with them, she grew up with the dream of being the best fairy in the world.

However, Caroline began to worry as the years passed, and she was left alone in the forest. Lula was the first to leave—a little girl was waiting for her in the very distant kingdom of Burkingtom, where women grow up to become warriors. A tough task awaited Lula because, surely, her daughter would have to face many dangers, so they all wished her good luck. The second to leave was Veronique— her daughter would be the queen of a very calm country that floated in the air, so her farewell was somewhat more joyous. Then Bennifer left— her child was a fire mage who was born blind, so he would have to help her not to burn everything by accident. Brittany left very excitedly because her daughter was an actress, and she wanted to see her first play. Monica left without warning.

One afternoon, Rome told Caroline that he had heard her little girl's call. She was on top of a great volcano— she was a girl chef who cooked with the fire of the volcano every time it erupted. Rome walked over to Caroline and gave her a big hug. Then she said,

"You are the best friend I have ever had, and it hurts a lot to leave you alone. I know that you will be the best fairy in the world. I hope you will soon feel the call of your girl."

Both fairies said goodbye between tears and joyful smiles. Rome left, and Caroline was left alone.

Many years passed, and Caroline became a true fairy lady. She had become the teacher of the little newborn fairies while she waited for her girl's call to appear finally.

"Your little girl must have grown into an adult by now, Caroline," Master Brume told Caroline.

"Yes… why is it that you still haven't called me? Could it be that she doesn't love me?"

"My dear, there are many reasons why that can happen."

"Really? Please tell me. I need it!

"Girls' hearts only call out to their fairies when they know the time is right. Remember, Caroline—it is the hearts of girls who call us, not girls. Their hearts are wiser than their heads; that's why we only obey him."

"I understand, but why are you not with your girl?"

"Her heart never caught me, my dear. I got tired of waiting and assumed it would never happen. That is why I dedicate myself to training the new fairies," said Master Brume sadly.

Caroline was horrified. Although she liked being a teacher, she couldn't imagine living her entire life without getting to know her little girl. The next morning, Caroline took all her things and fled the forest— she had decided to search for her girl by herself until she finds her. She would not wait to be called, nor live to wait for her fate!

Caroline began to travel around the world. She visited the paradisiacal beaches of Fruitlonge, asking the mermaids if they had heard of a girl who did not have a fairy. She ventured into the extremely beautiful jungle of the Biting Indians. She traveled the desert until she found the hidden Kingdom among the sands. She had lunch with the seals and the snowmen in the distant frozen country. But in none of those places, she managed to obtain clues as to her little girl's whereabouts!

On one of her trips, Caroline met Monica again, her old fairy friend when they were girls in the woods. Monica's child was a fortune-teller—an expert in the art of fortune-telling using her magic ball.

"Hello, Caroline!"

"Hello, Monica!"

Both fairies hugged with all the strength that their plump little bodies could reach without breaking their small and thin bones.

"Friend, I have excellent news for you! I tried to go tell you to the fairy forest as soon as I found out, but when I returned, you had already left."

"What do you have to tell me?"

"My girl has seen you, Caroline, she has seen you saving a girl from a terrible evil that has caused her a lot of damage!

"Is it serious?"

Monica's girl approached where both fairies were. She took Caroline's hands and began to do her divination magic.

"Caroline, the lovely and lonely fairy! Fate has waited for you for a long time, but you have not been able to hear the call!"

"Why? Is something wrong with me?"

"No, Caroline! A Witch cast a terrible spell on your child and silenced her heart. That is the reason why you could not hear her!"

Caroline fell to the ground to cry. The crying of the fairies was terribly high. It was as if they were furiously scratching a hundred slates. The worst thing that could happen to a person was to have their heart silenced. Not only was the opportunity to make a call to the destined fairy lost, but it would not be possible to show beautiful feelings, such as mercy, forgiveness, affection, or love.

"Tell me where it is! I will travel to break that spell immediately."

Monica and her little girl fortune-teller revealed to Caroline that their destined child was none other than the beautiful Princess of the great Kingdom of Mobgrinham and that her name was Diane. Everyone in the world knew Diane for being shy as a rabbit, cruel as a snake, and quiet as the night.

Caroline left like a flash. She couldn't let his little girl suffer for not knowing how to make her heart speak. She flew like a meteor through the skies with all the speed that her little fairy wings allowed her, and quite quickly, she reached the great Kingdom of Mobgrinham— there her child destiny would finally await her.

Upon arrival, the first thing she found out was that her daughter had been punished by her parents in a very, very high tower, in which she would have to stay locked up for having behaved insolently.

"I must get there. I must see her. I will know that she is my child when I see her eyes."

Caroline flew and flew high until she managed to find the tower where Princess Diane was. She found her crying, messy and dirty, lying on the feather bed, staring out the window. The Princess saw Caroline, and the fairy saw Diane—they felt nothing.

"What are you doing there spying on me, ugly fairy?" Diane told her.

"Hello, my name is Caroline, and I think you are my destined girl..."

"Get out of here and bother someone else! I am not anyone's destined girl. I have no destiny, nor do I feel like having it? Outside!" Diane yelled at Caroline.

The fairy did not expect anything different from their first meeting— she knew that this is how people who have mute hearts acted. She decided, then, to fly to the great castle of Mobgrinham to meet her parents. Arriving in front of them, she said:

"My King, my Queen! My name is Caroline, and I come to do what I should have done a long time ago."

"And what is that you come to do?" asked the King.

"I come to undo a terrible spell that has haunted your daughter from birth. I am Caroline, the fairy destined to protect Princess Diane, and today I come to discover who it was the Witch who made her heart mute!"

Everyone in the castle was horrified, the King even more.

"Are you telling us that our daughter has a dumb heart? That explains why she behaves the way she does!" said the King.

"Tell us, what can we do to help you?" asked the Queen.

"Do you have any idea who could be evil enough to bewitch your daughter?"

At that moment, all the light in the castle vanished. A shadow leaned out of each window of the building, and then they heard the most terrible of laughter in that place. A crow flew in through the door.

"I was the one who bewitched Princess Diane," said the Raven.

Suddenly, the blackbird was enveloped in a green cloud, which caused its legs to become legs, its feathers to become a garment, and its beak to transform into a mouth. When they realized it, the Raven was now a horrible older woman.

"Wow, ha, ha, ha! It was me who silenced the heart of that ugly girl when she was born. I am June, the Witch of disasters, and I did it because I want to become the owner of this entire Kingdom!"

Caroline took out her fairy wand and brought light back to the entire castle. The King looked at the Witch June and said:

"Old hag, give a voice back to our little Diane's heart!"

"I will do it on one condition," the Witch said.

"Which?" asked the Queen.

"You must give me your crowns and kneel before me! I want to be crowned the new Queen of Mobgrinham!"

Caroline stood in front of the Witch.

"Don't even think about it, my Kings, I'm here to do it any other way! I thought I would have to spend a lot more time looking for you, June, but you came here by yourself."

"You, little fairy, will you face me? I am the Witch of disasters. You will regret coming here!"

At that moment, June has enveloped in a green cloud again—her arms became giant wings, and her body took the form of a Dragon! The King and Queen fled with their soldiers. The Dragon Witch opened her mouth and breathed out the smelliest fire breath Caroline had ever seen. The fairy took her wand and created a magical barrier that protected her from the heat, then materialized a large pink hammer, and boom! She broke the teeth of the Dragon Witch with a great blow. Then it formed a gigantic web that pinned June to the ground. The Witch started crying because she knew she had lost, so she returned to her old woman form.

"Break the spell, Witch, or I'll turn you to dust!"

"Okay, okay!" There was silence. "Ready, I've already dissolved the spell!"

Caroline, the fairy, froze. The King and queen sent their soldiers to expel the Witch from their Kingdom, then met with Caroline.

"What is it, dear fairy? Why that strange face?"

Caroline felt joy coursing through her veins. She felt as if her head had finally found the direction it should go. It felt like the moon, and the sun had aligned, like her heart was pounding faster, and she was swimming in the most fantastic sea; like she was enjoying her favorite dish, and she felt her call finally come.

At that time, the soldiers returned to the castle.

"Your majesties, we have brought the Princess just as you requested!"

The beautiful Princess Diane entered the room, and the anger had disappeared from her gestures. There was no pain in her eyes. The fairy saw Diane, and the Princess saw Caroline, and they both felt it—they had finally met.

4 - Michael, the Squire, and the Rescue of the Princess

In a time so ancient that not even calendars go so far back in time, legend has it that a fearsome Dragon, as big as a castle and as mighty as a stampede, had trapped the most beautiful Princess of all, Lady Mary of

Zundor, because he wanted to take possession of everything that was beautiful in this world. All the knights of the planet spoke about this: The Dragon had to be defeated at any cost; the Princess needed to regain her freedom.

Although, everything seemed to indicate that this story would be like the others and that there would be a brave hero who would save the Princess from her terrible imprisonment with the Dragon, things were a bit different. The truth is that there was a hero, and his name is Michael. This is his story.

In those times, not just anyone could have the honor of being knighted. To be one, you had to be a warrior of extreme courage, possess the strength of ten bulls, have a fine education that would allow you to speak using strange words like 'magnificence' or at least be a handsome man willing to fight evil. Michael was none of this.

Michael was born in a very small and poor town called 'El Manure' because there were many animals there and always a bad smell. Our hero was not very strong, he had not been able to study, and he was not very handsome. He was an ordinary person, a fairly simple guy. However, fate smiled on Michael when one day, a great gentleman came to his town, named Sir Garelot, the Fantastic.

"I'm looking for a squire to have the honor of traveling with me around the world!" Sir Garelot announced.

Everyone in the small town lined up to prove their worth in front of the knight because no one wanted to live there their whole life. The only one who did not do it was Michael because he did not know about the arrival of the hero.

"Whoever manages to defeat the dark mule-man that lives in these lands and brings him here will become my squire!" Sir Garelot explained.

The mule-man was a fastidious and strong creature who lived near the town, known for throwing toilet paper on houses at night, singing so badly that flowers died of pain, and stealing tomatoes on farms. Everyone in the village tried to defeat him, but it was very difficult. The mule-man defeated them only by giving them a strong kick, and they all returned to the village crying for not having defeated him.

Sir Garelot could not believe that no one was able to defeat him:

"What is wrong with this town? It seems that there is no man brave enough to be my squire!" He said.

One of those days, the mule-man broke into Michael's farm to steal tomatoes. Our protagonist caught it on the spot and struck it so hard with his shovel that everyone in the Kingdom could hear the metallic echo. Michael dragged the passed out body of the mule-man and placed it in front of Sir Garelot, then said:

"I heard you were looking for this scoundrel. Take him out of here, please, I'm tired of him stealing from me!"

Sir Garelot was amazed:

"At last, someone worthy of traveling with me! What is your name, boy?" he asked.

"My name is Michael, and I don't know what trips you're talking about."

"Boy, from this day on, you will be known as Michael the Squire, and you will travel with me all over the world!"

51

"Great!" Michael said happily. He had managed to become a squire without knowing it.

Sir Garelot took Michael from his small town, and the two went on wild adventures. As part of his training, the knight had his squire face off alone against a hundred rabid goblins, while he sat watching him fight over an orange juice.

"Sir Garelot, I need your help!" Michael yelled at him as he felt crushed by the goblins.

"None of that, you must learn to fight! If I participate, the battle will be over in a minute, and that would not be fun at all," Sir Garelot replied.

In all the training Michael underwent to learn to fight, he never saw Sir Garelot raise his sword or fight an evil monster. Michael thought his teacher was lazy, but he couldn't tell him because it would send him back to his boring town!

On one of their many journeys, Michael and Sir Garelot learned the sad story of Lady Mary, the Princess of Zundor, who had been captured by the fearsome Dragon on top of a mountain so high that the clouds had to look up to be able to reach its peak with the sight.

"We should head over there right now, Michael! Said Sir Garelot. "That poor Princess must be suffering too much, alone up there!" Also, I have heard that she is gorgeous and that she is the heir to the Kingdom of Zundor after her parents died. She must be looking for a hero to save her and then make him her husband!"

Michael had heard many terrible things about the Dragon and the Princess. Therefore, he replied:

"Sir Garelot, are you sure we should get involved in this? No one has returned from this difficult task! We could find a Dragon too big for the two of us, or a mountain too difficult to climb."

Sir Garelot replied:

"That is nonsense, Michael. It should excite you more that no one has succeeded yet. If we succeed, we will become legends, and everyone will know our names!"

Michael replied:

"It doesn't interest me that they know my name. The only thing I want is to live in peace and help as much as I can."

"Perfect, then help me where you can and stop complaining so much!"

The squire and his knight finally began their journey up the shadowy mountain. On the way, they crossed a jungle where there were many covens of child-eating Witches, whom Michael defeated by teaching them that a vegetarian diet was more nutritious. They also crossed a bridge as long as two continents over a canyon as deep as a black hole. Sir Garelot spent the whole way singing some funny songs about how beautiful it was to be a knight, while Michael was the one who carried all the luggage, led the horses, planned the route, and prepared each of the meals. One day, both travelers realized that they had arrived.

"Look, Michael, that has to be the mountain!" Sir Garelot said as he pointed to the incredible dark structure that must have been at least 100 cities high, disappearing into the sky.

"Rewind! Is that what we are supposed to climb?"

"Yes, get ready, it will be a very interesting climb!"

Michael and Sir Garelot began to climb the terrible mountain. As they did so, a storm uglier than scolding broke out in the dark sky, drenching them completely, making the stones slippery and giving them an unpleasant chill that felt like a shower of wasps stinging all over their bodies. It took six days and 15 hours to climb, but in the end, they made it to the top. What they found there was incredible.

At first, they noticed the Dragon. Legends said it was as big as a castle and as powerful as a stampede, but they had fallen short. If that Dragon spread its wings and flew across the sky, many realms would be swallowed up by the shadow of its body. He was red like fire and had brown eyes like tree bark. However, what ended up drawing their attention was the beautiful Princess who was next to the Dragon, stroking its head.

"Be careful, fair lady, that Dragon can eat you!" shouted Sir Garelot recklessly.

"Don't be stupid, Sir Garelot! Now it will know we are here!"

The Dragon then spread its wings and showed its sharp teeth, then screamed at them:

"Who is the intruder who dares to come to my domain? Let her name say, or I will turn her to ashes with my breath of flames!"

Sir Garelot jumped in front of the Dragon and said:

"We are Sir Garelot, the fantastic and Michael, the squire, and we both came to defeat you to save that beautiful Princess!"

The Princess wanted to avoid a fight, so she said:

"Please stop, this is all a mistake!"

Sir Garelot did not listen to what the Princess was trying to say and continued to argue with the Dragon.

"Malignant winged serpent, today you will taste the taste of defeat!"

"Come to me, then fight me!"

"I'd rather you give up, so no one would have to witness Sir Garelot the fantastic humiliating a poor Dragon who couldn't behave!"

"Apologize, or I will cremate you!"

"Apologies are for cowards! Give up, or I'll beat you!"

They both argued and argued, like parrots. Michael took advantage of the Dragon's carelessness and approached Lady Mary.

"Hello, Princess."

"Hello, Michael the Squire"

"Could you explain what you were saying earlier? Why was coming here to save you a mistake?"

Lady Mary began to speak, and what she said was incredible:

"I am not imprisoned here as the rumors say; I am here because I need to be protected! Many years ago, a terrible dark spirit called Badsoul approached the castle, where I lived in peace with my parents, and promised that he would send an entire army of undead to destroy the entire kingdom. Then he said that when he finished, he would take me as his wife. Badsoul kept her promise, he attacked with everything he had and ended up destroying everything I knew and loved.

Except for my mother and me. My father died fighting alongside our people; we managed to escape."

"And where is your mother?" Michael asked.

Lady Mary pointed her finger at the Dragon and said:

"She's my mother! We have had the blood of Dragons in our veins for centuries. She transformed into one when she felt that we needed to be protected."

At that moment, Michael went to Sir Garelot and said:

"Sir Garelot, stop this absurd discussion now!"

Michael was about to tell her what he had learned, but suddenly the sky darkened. A terrible laugh began to be heard in the air, then it was heard:

"I finally managed to find you, Princess!"

Lady Mary and her dragon mother looked at each other and were very afraid. Then the Princess screamed:

"Oh no, it's Badsoul, he managed to find out where we were!"

Sir Garelot didn't even understand what was happening.

"Bad what? What is the Princess talking about?"

"Be quiet and watch out, we may have to participate in the greatest battle this world has ever seen, Sir Garelot!" Michael told him.

An immense wave of undead appeared on the top of the mountain, and they kept climbing higher and higher. Flying vampires with hideous wings appeared in the sky.

"Please guys, I need your help, I don't think I can beat everyone!" the Dragon mother said.

At that moment, Sir Garelot fell unconscious—he had not been able to with the nerves. Michael took him to the Princess, took up his magnificent knightly weapons, and then said:

"My Dragon queen, I will stand with you to defend Princess Mary until my last breath. Take care of those who fly. I'll have a party with those who come up!"

Then the Dragon flew through the air and faced the thousands of vampires who threatened to take her daughter. Michael, the Squire, steeled himself and fought against the thousands of skeletons as if he were a thousand men instead of one. The fight lasted three days and five hours until Badsoul appeared, and the hordes of the undead stopped attacking.

"My Princess, my dear Princess! Why don't you stop this mess now and join me of your own free will? I will spare the life of the Dragon and this squire if you do."

Michael interrupted him:

"On my corpse, you will never touch the Princess's hair!"

Then the squire ran with the energy he had left to try to unleash a sword blow to the evil spirit. Still, Badsoul was magical and powerful, so with opening his mouth and blowing into the wind, Michael shot backward, falling unconscious next to Lady Mary. Badsoul raised his hands, and bolts shot out of them, striking the Dragon, causing her to collapse on top, along with Michael and Lady Mary.

"You are alone, little one! Come with me, or I'll take your life," Badsoul told him.

However, at that moment, the most unexpected hero appeared—Sir Garelot, the fantastic, would save the day!

"Silly creature, never turn your back on your opponent!" he said just before pushing him off the top of the mountain.

"No, no, no, no, no...!" It was heard as the spirit fell to the bottom. Not even he would be able to survive the fall.

A long time has passed since Badsoul's defeat. Next, Lady Mary, Michael, and their mother flew through the heavens and returned to the realm that once destroyed the evil being. There, a great party was organized that was full of Kings, queens, and Princes from all over the world. They were celebrating because the Queen and Lady Mary had come home! The Princess decided that it was time for the main act of the event—the consecration of Michael as a knight.

"Dear Michael, great hero...!"

Sir Garelot interrupted from the background:

"I was the hero, I was the one who killed Badsoul!" but nobody was paying attention.

The Princess continued:

"You fought alongside my mother as the bravest hero of all. From today you will be known as Michael the Magnificent, and you will be my protective knight!"

After that, everyone lived happily in the Kingdom of Zundor. Michael ended up marrying the Princess after ten years and became King. Sir Garelot never stopped telling that the monarch was once his squire.

5 - Ferland, the Ghost, and the Witch

It tells a story that many years ago, when there were still Dragons, Witches, and goblins inhabiting this world as if it were their playground. A little ghost named Ferland appeared in the distant Kingdom of Brunmor, who was quite sad because he did not know how he had died.

"What do I do here? Why don't I know who I was or why I died? I hardly know my name!" poor Ferland wondered.

Our ghost friend came into existence one day when the whole sky turned like gold, and a strong and cold breeze stirred the hearts of the inhabitants of that Kingdom. Ferland appeared out of nowhere in a small town called Mambur, and his body was so strange that anyone who had seen him might have passed out from the shock. It was as if a white blob, with a child's face and eyes as blue as the sea, was floating through the air. A ghost like him had never been seen. Others used to have terrible appearances, voices as unpleasant as fingernails on the blackboard, and a very bad mood. Ferland was very different, it was as if a very good child has had his body taken away and left flying through the air, which made him very sad.

Although at first everyone in Mambur had been afraid to see him, he soon became friends with all the inhabitants. A big-hearted lady, named Melany the Wise, had taken it upon herself to adopt him so he wouldn't have to wander alone and helpless. Melany loved him very much, and always told him:

"Little Ferland, my beloved ghost, don't be sad! You have many friends here in Mambur who appreciate you because we know that you are good. The day will come when you will be able to remember who you were, and we will all have a party to celebrate it!"

Ferland had two great friends in that town— their names were Raven and Benja. Raven was the son of a great knight who served the King of Brunmor in his incredible castle, so he always had great stories of his father to tell. Raven told them:

"My dad is the best gentleman of all time! The last time he came here, he told me that he faced ten snakes as fat as cows and as long as a river, defeating them without shedding a drop of sweat. He also saved a hundred Princesses from a hideous ogre who had locked them in a cage inside a dark cave— he made that ogre faint with fear just by showing his incredible silver sword!"

Ferland told him with some sadness:

"Friend, how does it feel to have a warrior father? I don't remember how it feels to have a father."

Raven replied:

"I am very proud to be his son. He is a true champion! The only problem is that he is always traveling and facing very dangerous creatures, and that worries me because I do not see him much. It has been almost a year since the last time he was with me. You had not appeared at that time."

Benja said to Raven:

"Dude, sometimes it's okay that your parents aren't home! So you can learn to grow by yourself, and you don't have someone behind you all the time."

Benja's father was a very loving and kind man named Dylan. He worked as an inventor and was known throughout the Kingdom for his creativity. He once managed to create a potion to make cows grow wings for a few minutes. On another occasion, he invented a fiery sword used by the Knights of Brunmor to face the terrible snowmen. What bothered Benja a little was that her father was always at home and that he never gave her space to have adventures with her friends.

"You should both be happy, at least you know who your fathers are!" poor Ferland told them.

The three friends had many fun adventures together. Taking advantage of Ferland's ability to fly and go through walls, they once managed to scare an evil teacher from her school into believing that an evil spirit had entered her house. They also played hide and seek all over town, and Ferland always won because he knew how to make himself invisible.

On one occasion, the three of them managed to prevent a fire in their village. This was what happened:

A scream as ugly as a stomach ache and as loud as a storm was heard at the entrance to the town of Mambur. It was a man who ran down the road while sobbing in pain and was on fire. Everyone in town was scared because the poor man was causing the houses there to start to catch fire. Despite everyone telling the man to calm down and stop running so he could put out the fire, he was not listening. He was saying:

"I can't stop running; the Witch told me that if I do, I will finish burning!"

Dylan, Benja's father, came up with a solution. He told Ferland:

"Little ghost, I have created an invention called 'hose' that serves so that the water of a pond can be shot in another place! I need you to go up to heaven with it and from there put out all the fire in the place."

"Yes, sir, I'm on it!" Ferland replied.

The inventor then told his son and Raven:

"Boys, I need you to use your strength to form a path with stones that the burning man can travel without continuing to burn the town and without stopping running."

"It's okay!" both friends told him.

Soon Benja and Raven put together a long labyrinth-like path, where the poor burning man found himself locked in while Ferland doused the fires from the sky. When the fire was finally extinguished, the ghost used all the water in the pool to put out the burning man.

"Thanks, I thought I was going to roast like a chicken!" said the poor man.

Melany knew him, and the rest of the town walked over to where he was. The older woman asked him:

"Why were you on fire? How come you didn't burn out completely? You almost wiped out our town!"

The man replied:

"Dear people of Mambur, I am very sorry! My name is Bestur, and I am a knight of the order of the King of Brunmor. I was lit in those terrible flames for a month because of the spell of an evil Witch who captured all my companions except me. I ran and ran all over the world because she assured me that if I stopped running, the fire would kill me. I came here because the leader of our order of knights, Dave the Mighty, told me that an inventor named Dylan lived here and would be able to rescue them and put them out my flames, and why should I warn little Raven that his father was in trouble."

Raven became very concerned with Bestur the knight's words:

"It can't be, is my father captured? We must go rescue him from the clutches of that Witch!"

Benja's father asked the knight:

"What were the knights doing confronting that Witch?"

Bestur, the knight replied:

"The King ordered us to go to his lair, in the terrible Goldblood Wilderness, to rescue his son. The Witch kidnapped the little Prince a few months ago, so we went there to give her what she deserved."

Then Dylan, the inventor, began to prepare his best creations for the fearsome confrontation that would come against the evil Witch. Benja, Raven, and Ferland told him:

"We want to go with you. We also want to defeat that Witch and save Raven's father!"

Dylan, the inventor, replied:

"Okay, you can, but you must promise me that you will not fight any Witch! Remember that Bestur and I are the adults, and that we are the ones who will take the risk in battle. Promise it?"

"We promise!" they said. However, Benja, Raven, and Ferland, the ghost, crossed their fingers.

Before leaving, Ferland went to where he lived with Melany the wise and said:

"Melany, you have been like my mother since I came here. Thank you for taking care of me, protecting me, and keeping me company even though I am a ghost. I love you very much; soon I will return, wanting to see you again."

"Dear Ferland, I hope that traveling helps you regain the memories of your past. Take care!" she said him back.

The five heroes left for the desert, where the wicked Witch held the knights and the little son of the King of Brunmor. They traveled for ten days and ten nights. Ferland, the ghost, was very happy because he was slowly recovering his memories with each landscape he saw. It was as if he had already visited all those lands, as if he knew all the ways of the Kingdom.

When they reached the desert, it took them two days to find their way to the cave where the Witch had her lalr. Since everyone was thirsty, Ferland flew and flew across the desert to find springs where they could recover and drink water. After much walking, Bestur, the knight shouted:

"Look, there is the Witch's lair!" and they all looked on in amazement. The place looked as if the desert had opened a huge mouth, so dark that the sunlight had to ask permission to peek inside. Dylan, the inventor, gave his companions glasses, except Ferland, because he did not need them to see what was inside without light torches.

When they entered the lair, the terrible smell of evil and vinegar caused their bones and ectoplasm to shake. Bestur led them to the cells where the knights were. When Raven saw his father, he screamed:

"Dad, you're here, I'm glad you're alive!"

Dave, the Mighty replied to his son:

"What the hell are you doing here, Raven? This is the most dangerous place in the whole world; you shouldn't have come!"

"We have come to rescue you!"

At that moment, Ferland, the ghost, and his friends heard the terrible sound of a Witch's laugh.

"Ha, ha, ha, ha! They made the mistake of coming here. Now I will have more souls to feed on!"

Ferland decided to make his body invisible. At that moment, the ugliest Witch ever born in the entire world appeared to the heroes. She looked as if a green snake had grown arms, her nose was like a toucan's, and her voice sounded like a flute completely out of tune.

"I love when more prey comes to me. I will have food for many months!"

Dylan, the inventor, was fearless, so he asked her:

"Do you eat souls, evil Witch?"

"Yes, they are my favorite food!"

"Then why haven't you eaten any of these gentlemen?"

"I'll tell you because I'm going to lock you all up! Many months ago, I kidnapped the King's son, little Ferland, and since then, I have been trying to feed on his soul, but the blood of Kings is very powerful, even against my magic! The boy's soul managed to escape, and I am using all my power to bring it back."

Everyone remained in silence. Ferland couldn't believe it, he was the King's son!

"Enough of the chatter, time to destroy you!" said the Witch

At that time, Dyland, the inventor, brought out his latest creation, a vacuum cleaner capable of absorbing any spell. With it, he managed to prevent the Witch from setting them on fire. Benja and Raven took the anti-witch nets that Dylan had made, and with them, they captured the villain. Bestur, the knight took her silver sword and said to the Witch:

"This is what happens when you burn a man and force him to run for a whole month!" and he hit her so hard that it made her disappear.

Everyone in the place celebrated and soon released the knights who were locked up, but no one was able to find Ferland.

"Where are you, Ferland? They all shouted."

When they plunged deeper into the depths of the Witch's lair, they found it. Little Ferland had managed to regain his body and was trying to support himself on his legs, but he was so weak that he could leave at any moment.

"Let's go back to our King, there we will save the little Prince!" the knights yelled.

The large group sped out of the desert, reaching the vast Brunmor Castle in less than a breath.

The great King Garret summoned his best magicians and physicians, and they made little Ferland survive.

When the Prince woke up, he found that everyone in the castle had thrown a big party to receive him. All the inhabitants of the town of Mambur were there, and they gave him the strongest of hugs when they saw him leave his room. Melany, the wise, kissed his forehead and said:

"Dear Ferland, in the end, you were not dead! I'll tell you what, you were adorable as a ghost, but now you are even more handsome," and they both smiled with joy.

The King went to his son and said:

"Without you here, I felt that my world was over, my son. How glad I am to know that you were alive and that you never surrendered against that Witch! Even being a ghost, you were a hero."

After that, all of Ferland's friends went to live with him in the castle. Melany became her nanny, and Dyland, the inventor, built the largest Kingdom's factories. Finally, they all managed to be happy forever.

6 - The Fairy of the Cascade

In the center of the great hall of the castle of Mystikland, King Altair was seated in a green reed chair, upon which a fire-colored silk cover and a red satin cushion were thrown under his elbow. With him were his knights Alphonse, Kyro, and Kiu, while at the other end, near the window, were Hecate, the queen, and her maidens, embroidering white clothes with strange gold devices.

"I'm tired," said Altair, "and until my food is ready, I'll have a sleep of pleasure. You can tell each other stories yourself, and Kiu will fetch you a jar of juice and some meat from the kitchen."

And after eating and drinking, Kyro, the oldest among them, began his story.

"I was the only child of my father and mother, and they gave me a lot of importance, but I was not content to stay with them at home, because I thought that no action in the whole world was too powerful for me. Nobody was able to contain me, and, after winning many adventures in my own land, I said goodbye to my parents and left to see the world. I crossed mountains, deserts, and rivers, until I came to a beautiful valley full of trees, with a path that ran beside a stream. I walked that path all day, and at night I came to a castle in front of two young men dressed in yellow, each holding an ivory bow, with arrows made from whale bones and winged with peacock feathers. Beside them, gold daggers hung with fists from whale bones.

Next to these young people was a richly dressed man, who turned and went with me towards the castle, where all the residents were gathered in the hall. In a window, I saw twenty-four maidens, and the least beautiful of them was more beautiful than Hecate at her most good-looking. Some of them took my horse, and others unbuckled my armor and washed it, with my sword and spear, until everything shone like silver. Then I washed and put on a vest and a doublet that was brought to me, and the man who entered with me and I sat at a silver table, and a most beautiful banquet I have ever had.

All this time, neither the man nor the maidens had spoken a word, but when our dinner was over, and my hunger subsided, the man began to ask who I was. So I told him my name and my father's name and why I came there because, in fact, I was tired of gaining dominion over all the men at home, and I looked to see if by chance there was anyone who could gain dominion about me. And with that, the man smiled and replied:

"If I weren't afraid to upset you too much, I would show you what you're looking for." His words made me sad and afraid of myself, which the man realized and added: "If you really want to say what you say, and sincerely want to prove your worth, and do not brag in vain that no one can beat you, I have something to show you. But tonight you must sleep in this castle, and in the morning see that you get up early and follow the road up through the valley until you reach a forest.

There is a path in the forest that branches to the right; follow this path until you reach a space of grass with a mound in the middle. At the top of the mound is a black man, bigger than any two white men, his eye is in the center of his forehead, and he has only one foot. It carries an iron club, and two white men could barely lift it. A thousand animals graze around him, all of the different types, because he is the guardian of that forest, and it is he who will tell you which way to go in order to find the adventure you are looking for."

So said the man, and that night seemed long to me, and before dawn, I got up and put on my armor, and mounted my horse and rode until I reached the grassy space he had told me about. There was the black man at the top of the hill, as he had said, and he was actually more powerful in every way than I thought he was. As for the club, Kiu, it would have been a heavy load for four of our soldiers. He waited for me to express myself, and I asked what power he had over the beasts that crowded so close to him.

"I will show you, little man," he replied, and with his club, he hit a deer on the head until it brayed loudly. And with their bray, the animals came running, numerous as the stars in the sky, so that I could barely get between them. Serpents were also there, and dragons and beasts of strange shapes, with horns in places where I had never seen horns before. And the black man just looked at them and told them to eat. And they fell down before him, like vassals before their master.

"Now, little man, I answered your question and showed you my power," he said. "Is there anything else you would like to know?" So I asked him my way, but he was angry and, as I realized, he would have gladly stopped me, but in the end, after I told him who I was, his anger passed him.

Then, he continued, "And the moment your song sounds sweetest, you will hear a murmur and complaint coming towards you along the valley, and you will see a black velvet rider riding a black horse, carrying a spear with a black streamer, and he will spur your steed to fight with you. If you turn to run, he will catch up. And if you remain where you are, he will dismantle you. And if you find no problems with this adventure, you don't have to look for them for the rest of your life."

So, I said goodbye to him and went up to the top of the forest, where I found everything as they had told me. I went to the tree under which the Cascade was, filled the silver bowl with water, and emptied it onto the marble slab. Then, thunder came much louder than I expected to hear, and after the thunder came rain much heavier than I expected to feel, because, in truth, I tell you, Kiu, none of those hailstones would be blocked by skin or flesh until it reaches the bone. I turned my horse's side towards the shower and, bending over his neck, held my shield so that I could cover his head and mine. When the hail passed, I looked at the tree, and not a single leaf remained on it, and the sky was blue, and the sun was shining.

I was listening to the birds, when, behold, a murmuring voice approached me, saying:

"Oh gentleman, what brought you here? What harm did I do to you that you would wish to do to me? Never, in all my lands, neither man nor animal that faced that rain escaped alive." Then, from the valley, the rider appeared on the black horse, holding the spear with the black pennant. We immediately attacked each other, and although I fought my best, he soon beat me, and I was terrified to the ground, though the rider grabbed my horse's bridle and left with him, leaving me where I was, without even divesting myself of my armor.

Unfortunately, I went down the hill again, and when I got to the clearing where the black man was, I confess to you, Kiu, it was a wonder that I didn't melt in a liquid pool, so great was my shame. That night, I slept in the castle where I had been before, showered, and partied, and no one asked me how I had been. The next morning, when I got up, I found a bay horse saddled for me and, wrapped in my armor, I came back to my own court. The horse was still in the stable, and I would not be separated from him by anyone in the hills.

Bul in truth, Kiu, no man has ever confessed an adventure so much to his own dishonor, and strange, in fact, it seems that no other man I have ever met who knew the black man, and the knight and the shower.

"Wouldn't it be nice," said Alphonse, "to go and find the place?"

"By the hand of my friend," replied Kiu, "you often pronounce with your tongue what you do not want to repair with your actions."

"Actually," said the queen's Hecate, who had heard the story, "you would be better hanged, Kiu, than talking to a man like Alphonse like that."

"I didn't mean anything, madam," replied Kiu; "your compliment to Alphonse is no higher than mine." And while he was talking, Altair woke up and asked if he hadn't slept a bit.

"Yes, sir," Alphonse replied, "you certainly slept."

"Is it time for us to eat meat?", asked the king.

"That's true, sir," Alphonse replied.

Then the horn for washing was sounded, and after that, the king and his family sat down to eat. And when they were done, Alphonse left them and got his horse and weapons ready.

With the first glimmers of the sun, he set and traveled through deserts, mountains and rivers, and everything that had happened to Kyro fell on him, until he was under the leafless tree listening to the birds singing. After that, he perceived the voice and, turning off to look, found the horseman galloping to meet him. They fought fiercely until their spears were broken, and then they drew their swords, and a blow from Alphonse cut the knight's helmet and knocked him off the horse.

Feeling wounded to death, the knight fled, and Alphonse pursued him until they reached a splendid castle. Here the rider crossed the bridge and the ditch, and reached the gate, but when he was safely inside, the drawbridge pulled and caught Alphonse's horse in the middle, so that half was in and half was outside, and Alphonse couldn't dismount and didn't know what to do.

While he was in this difficult situation, a small door at the castle gate opened, and he could see a street in front of him, with tall houses. Then, a maiden with golden curly hair looked through the door and asked Alphonse to open the gate.

"For my faith!" shouted Alphonse, "I cannot open it from here anymore than you are able to free me."

"Well," she said, "I will do my best to free you if you do what I tell you. Take this ring and put it with the stone in your hand and close your fingers tightly, because while you hide it, it will hide you. When the men inside meet, they will come and fetch you to trap you and will be very sad not to find you . I will be on the horse block there, and you can see me, although I cannot see you. So come over and put your hand on my shoulder and follow me wherever I go."

After that, she moved away from Alphonse, and when the men left the castle to look for him and did not find him, they were deeply saddened and returned to the castle.

Then Alphonse went to the maiden and put his hand on his shoulder, and she led him into a large room, all painted in rich colors and adorned with gold images. Here she gave him food and drink, and water to wash and clothes to wear, and he lay down on a soft bed, covered in scarlet and fur, and slept happily.

At midnight, he woke up to a loud cry, and he jumped and dressed and went into the room, where the maiden was stand-up.

"What is it?" he asked, and she replied that the knight who owned the castle was dead, and they were taking his body to the church. Never before had Alphonse seen such a vast crowd, and following the dead knight was the most beautiful fairy in the world, whose cry was louder than the cry of men or the bray of trumpets. And Alphonse looked at her and loved her.

"Who is she?" he asked the maiden. "This is my Fairy, the countess of the Cascade, and the wife of the one you killed yesterday."

"Actually," said Alphonse, "she is the woman I love the most."

"She will also love you little," said the maiden.

So she left Alphonse, and after a while, she went to her mistress's room and spoke to her, but the countess answered nothing.

"What's going on, Fairy?" asked the maiden.

"Why did you stay away from me in my pain, Luned?" replied the countess, and in turn, the maiden asked:

"Is it good for you to cry so bitterly for the dead, or for anything that is gone from you?"

"There is no man in the world like him," replied the countess, her face red with anger. "I would like to banish to you because of those words."

"Don't be mad, madam," said Luned, "but listen to my advice. You know very well that alone you cannot preserve your lands, so look for someone to help you."

"And how can I do that?" asked the countess.

"I'll tell you," said Luned. "Unless you can defend the source, all will be lost, and no one will be able to defend the source except a knight from Altair's court. There I will look for him and woe to me if I return without a warrior who can guard the Cascade, just like the one who kept it before."

"Go then," said the countess, "and prove what you promised."

So Luned left, riding on a white palfrey, under the pretext of traveling to King Altair's court, but instead of doing so, she hid for as many days as it would take to come and go, and then she left her hiding place and went to the countess.

"What's the news from the court?" Asked his mistress when she gave Luned a warm greeting.

"The best news," replied the maiden, "because I have achieved the objective of my mission. When do you want me to introduce you to the knight who came back with me?"

"Tomorrow at noon," said the countess, "and I will make all the townspeople come together."

So the next day, at noon, Alphonse put on his chain mail and a splendid cloak over it, while on his feet were leather shoes fastened with gold buckles. And he followed Luned to his Fairy's chamber.

The Countess was very happy to see them, but she looked at Alphonse carefully and said:

"Luned, this knight barely looks like a traveler."

"What's wrong with that, Fairy?" Replied Luned.

"I am convinced," said the countess, "that this man and no other has expelled the soul from my lord's body."

"If he were no stronger than your lord," replied the maiden, "he might not waste his life, and all effects that have passed, there is no remedy."

"Leave me, you two," said the countess, "and I will advise you."

So they left. In the morning, the countess summoned her subjects to gather in the castle's courtyard and expressed to them that now that her spouse was gone, there was no one to defend their land.

"Then choose what it will be," she said. "Let one of you take me as your wife or give me your consent to take a new lord for me, lest my lands are left without a lord."

Upon hearing her words, the city chiefs retreated to a corner and counseled, and after a while, the leader stepped forward and said that they had decided that it was best, for the peace and security of all, that she choose a husband for herself same. Then Alphonse was called into her presence and gladly accepted the hand she offered him, and they were married immediately, and the men of the county paid homage to him.

From that day on, Alphonse defended the Cascade as the earl before him had done, and he defeated all passing knights and his ransom divided among his barons. In that way, three years passed, and no man in the world was more loved than Alphonse.

Then, at the end of three years, it happened that the knight Gwalchmai was with Altair, and he realized that the king was very sad.

"My lord, did something happen to you?" he asked.

"Oh, Gwalchmai, I am sorry for Alphonse, to whom I lost those three years, and if a fourth year goes by without him, I cannot live any longer. And I'm sure that the story told by Kyro, son of Clydno, made me lose him. I myself will go with the men in my house to avenge him if he is dead, to release him if he is in prison, to bring him back if he is alive."

So Altair and three thousand men from his home set out to find Alphonse and took Kyro as a guide. When Altair arrived at the castle, the young men were shooting at the same place, and the same yellow man was nearby, and as soon as he saw Altair, he greeted him and invited him in, and they went in together. The castle was so vast that the king's three thousand men were worth no more than if they were twenty.

At dawn, Altair left there, with Kyro as his guide, and reached the black man first, and then the top of the wooded hill, with the Cascade, the bowl, and the tree.

"My lord," said Kiu, "let me throw the water on the slab and receive the first adventure that can happen."

"You can do that," said Altair, and Kiu splashed the water.

92

Everything immediately happened as before; the thunder and hail that killed many of Altair's men; the song of birds, and the appearance of the black knight. And Kiu found him and fought, and was knocked down by him. The knight left then, and Altair and his men camped where they were.

In the morning, Kiu again excused himself to find the knight and try to beat him, which Altair granted. But again, he was dismounted, and with a humble spirit, he returned to the camp.

After that, each of the knights fought, but none won, and in the end, only Altair and Gwalchmai remained.

"Oh, let me fight him, my lord," cried Gwalchmai, seeing Altair taking him in his arms.

"Well, fight then," said Altair, and Gwalchmai threw a tunic over himself and his horse so that no one knew him. They fought all that day, and neither managed to overthrow the other and so it was the following day. On day number three, the combat was so violent that both fell to the ground at the same time and fought on their feet, and at last, the black knight gave his enemy a blow so hard on the head that his helmet fell from his face.

"I didn't know it was you, Gwalchmai," said the black knight. "Take my sword and my arms."

"No," replied Gwalchmai, "it is you, Alphonse, the winner, take my sword," but Alphonse didn't.

"Give me your swords," said Altair behind them, "because neither of you beat the other," and Alphonse turned and put his arms around Altair's neck.

The next day, Altair reportedly ordered his men to prepare to return where they came from, but Alphonse stopped him.

"My noble," he said, "during the three years that I was absent from you, I have prepared a feast for you, knowing full well that you would come looking for me. So stay with me for a while, you and your men."

So they rode to the Countess's castle at the Cascade and spent three months resting and partying. And when it was time for them to leave, Altair pleaded with the countess to allow Alphonse to go with him to the hills for the space of three months. With a sore heart, she decided to give permission, and Alphonse was so pleased to be with his old companions again that three years instead of three months passed like a dream.

One day Alphonse sat at the table in Mystikland's castle in Usk, when a maiden on a bay horse arrived in the hall and, riding straight to the place where Alphonse was sitting, she bent down and took the ring from his hand.

"So the traitor and the infidel will be treated," she said, turning the horse's head and leaving the hall.

With her words, Alphonse remembered everything he had forgotten and, sad and ashamed, went to his own room and prepared to leave. At dawn, he left but did not return to the castle, as his heart was heavy, but he wandered through wild places until his body was thin and thin, and his hair was long. The wild animals were his friends, and he slept beside them, but in the end, he wished to see a man's face again, and he went down to a valley and slept by a river in the lands of a widowed countess.

The time came when the countess took a walk, accompanied by her maids, and when they look at a man lying by the lake, they retreated in terror, for he was so still that they thought he was dead. But when they overcame fear, they approached him, and touched him, and saw that there was life in him. Then the countess hurried to the castle, brought him a vial full of valuable ointment, and gave it to one of her maids.

"Take that horse that is grazing there," she said, "and a suit of men's clothing, and place them next to the man, and pour some of this ointment near your heart. If there is any life in it, that will bring it back. But if he moves, hide in the nearby bushes and see what he does."

The maiden took the flask and did her mistress's orders. Soon the man started to move his arms and stood up slowly. Advancing step by step, he removed his robes from the saddle and placed them on him, and painfully he mounted the horse. When he was seated, the maiden came to greet him, and he was happy when he saw her and asked what castle was before him.

"It belongs to a widowed countess," replied the maiden. "Her husband left her two counties, but that is all that remains of her vast lands, as they were taken from her by a young count because she did not want to marry him."

"It's a shame," Alphonse replied, but said nothing more, as he was too weak to tell much. Then the maid guided him to the castle, lit a fire, and brought him food. And there he stayed and was cared for three months until he was more handsome than ever.

One day, at noon, Alphonse heard the sound of guns outside the castle and asked the maiden what it was.

"It was the count I spoke to you with," she replied, "who came with a large army to take my Fairy."

"Beg her to lend me a horse and armor," Alphonse said, and the maiden complied, but the countess laughed a little bitterly when she replied:

"No, but I will give him, and a horse, armor, and weapons that he never had yet, although I don't know what use they will have for him. However, perhaps it will save them from falling into the hands of my enemies."

The horse was brought in, and Alphonse rode with two pages behind him, and they saw the great army encamped before them.

"Where's the count?" he said, and the pages replied:

"In the troop, there are four yellow banners."

"Wait for me," said Alphonse, at the castle gate and shouted a challenge to the earl, who came to meet him. They fought hard, but Alphonse took down his enemy and pushed him in front of the castle gate into the hall.

"Here is the reward for your blessed balm," he said, as he ordered the count to kneel before her and made him swear that he would restore everything he had taken from her.

After that, he left and went into the desert, and as he passed through the woods, he heard a shout. Moving away from the bushes, he saw a lion standing on a large mound and, beside him, a rock. Near the rock, a lion was trying to reach the mountain, and each time it moved, a snake would shoot from the rock to stop it. Then Alfonso drew his sword, shooed the snake away and continued on his way, and the lion happily followed him as if it were his new pet. And he was much more useful than a greyhound because, at night, he brought large logs in his mouth to light the fire and killed a fat deer for dinner.

Alphonse lit the fire and removed the male's skin, put some to roast, and gave the lion the rest for dinner. While waiting for the meat to cook, he heard a deep sighing sound next to him, and he said:

"Who are you?"

"I'm Luned," answered a voice from a cave so hidden by bushes and hanging green plants that Alphonse hadn't seen it.

"And what are you doing here?" He shouted.

"I am trapped in this cave because of the knight who married the countess and left her, as the pages spoke ill of him, and as I told them that no man alive was his equal, they dragged me here and said that I should die unless he comes to set me free on a certain day, and that is no more than the day after tomorrow. His name is Alphonse, son of Urien, but I have no one to send to tell him about my danger or the assurance that he will deliver me."

Alphonse was silent but gave the maiden some of the meat and asked her to be of good cheer. Then, followed by the lion, he left for a huge palace on the other part of the plain, and all men came and took his horse and put him in a manger, and the lion went after him and lay down on the straw. Hospitable and kind people were all inside the castle, but so full of sadness that death seemed to be upon them. Finally, after eating and drinking, Alphonse prayed that the earl would tell him the reason for his pain.

"Yesterday," replied the count, "my two sons were captured while you were hunting, by a monster who lives in the mountains far away, and he swears that he will not let them go unless I give him my daughter as his wife."

"That will never be," said Alphonse, "but what shape does this monster have?"

"In form, he is a man, but in stature, he is a giant," replied the count, "and it would be far better for him to kill my children than for me to give up my daughter."

The next morning, the castle's residents were awakened by a great outcry and discovered that the enormous had arrived with the two young men. Alphonse quickly put on his armor and went out to meet the giant, and the lion followed him. And when the great beast saw the hard blows that the giant dealt on his master, he flew in his throat, and the monster had many problems to defeat him.

"Actually," said the giant, "I would have no trouble fighting with you if it weren't for that lion." When Alphonse learned of this, he felt ashamed of not being able to defeat the giant with his own blade, so he took the lion and locked it in one of the castle's towers, and give back to the fight. From the sound of the setbacks, the lion knew that the fight was going badly for Alphonse, so he climbed up to the top of the tower, where there was a door to the roof, and from the tower where he jumped the walls, and the walls to the ground. Then, with a loud roar, he jumped on the giant, who fell dead under the blow of his paw.

Now the castle's darkness turned to joy, and the count begged Alphonse to stay with him until he could make a feast, but the knight said he had another job to do and galloped back to the place where he had left Luned, and the lion followed on his heels. When he got there, he saw a big fire burning and two young men taking the maiden to throw it on the pile.

"Stop!" he shouted, running up to them. "What accusation do you have against her?"

"She swanked that no man in the world was like Alphonse," they said, "and we locked her up in a cave, and we agreed that no one should hand her over except Alphonse himself and that if he didn't come in one certain day, she must die. And now the time has passed, and there is no sign of it."

"Actually, he is a good knight, and if he knew that the maid was in danger, he would have risen to save her," said Alphonse, "but take me in your place, I beg you."

"Come on," they replied, and the fight started.

The young men fought well and put a lot of pressure on Alphonse, and when the lion realized that, came to help his master, the youth signaled for the fight to stop and said:

"Chief, it was agreed that we should only fight against you, and it is more difficult for us to fight that beast than with you."

Then Alphonse locked the lion in the cave where the maiden had been in prison and blocked the front with stones. But the fight with the giant had proved him a lot, and the youth fought well and pressed him harder than before. And when the lion saw it, it gave a great roar, burst through the stones, and leaped over the youth and killed them. And so Luned was finally delivered.

Then the maiden rode back with Alphonse to the land of the source Fairy. And he took the Fairy with him to Altair's court, where they lived happily ever after.

7 - The White Dog

Once upon a time in a beautiful far place, there was a king who had three children and, because they were all so good and handsome, he could not decide which one to give his kingdom. he was getting old and began to think that soon the time would come to choose one of them to rule in his place .

So he decided to give them a task to do, and what would be most successful would be to have the kingdom as a reward.

It took some time before he could decide what the task should be. But, at last, he told them that he liked a very cute horse and that everyone should go looking for one for him. They would have an entire year to search, and everyone should return to the castle on the same day and introduce the various horses they had chosen at the same time.

The three princes were very surprised by their father's sudden passion for a horse. Still, when they heard that any of them who brought the most beautiful little animal would be their father's successor on the throne, they no longer objected, as this gave them both younger children a chance that they would not otherwise have to be king.

Then they said goodbye to their father and, after agreeing to return to the castle at the same time and on the same day, when a year should have passed, the three brothers all started together.

Many lords and servants accompanied them out of the city. Still, after traveling about a league, they all sent back and, after hugging each other affectionately, all set out to try their luck in different directions.

The older two had many adventures on their travels, but the younger one saw the most wonderful landscapes of all.

He was young and handsome, also as brave and smart as a prince should be.

Wherever he went, he asked about horses, and hardly a day went by without him buying several, big and small, greyhounds, spaniels, lap horses, and colorful horses - in fact, all kinds of horses you can imagine. Very soon, he had a troop of fifty or sixty trotting after him, one of which he thought would surely win the prize.

Thus, he traveled day after day, not knowing where he was going, until one night he was lost in a dense and dark forest, and after wandering many kilometers, tired, in the wind and rain, he was glad to see a brilliant light shine. through the trees finally. He thought he must have been near a woodcutter's hut, but his surprise was when he found himself in front of the entrance to a splendid castle!

At first, he hesitated to enter, as the journey stained his robes, and he was soaked with rain so that no one could have noticed he was a prince. All the cute horses that he took the time to collect were lost in the forest, and he was completely tired and discouraged.

However, something seemed to invite him to enter the castle, so he pulled the bell. Immediately the portal opened, and several beautiful white hands appeared and waved him across the courtyard and into the great hall.

Here he found a splendid fire lit, next to which was a comfortable armchair; their hands pointed invitingly at him, and, as soon as the prince sat down, they began to take off his wet and muddy clothes and dress him in a magnificent silk and velvet suit.

When he was ready, the hands led him to a well-lit room, where a table was open for dinner. Finishing the room, there was a raised platform, on which several dogs were sitting, all playing different musical instruments.

The prince began to think that he must have been dreaming when the door opened, and a lovely white dog entered. She was dressed in a long black veil and was accompanied by several dogs, dressed in black and carrying swords.

She approached the prince directly and, in a sweet and sad little voice, welcomed him. Then she ordered dinner to be served, and the whole group sat down together.

Mysterious hands served them, but many of the dishes were not to the prince's liking. Cooked rats and mice can be a first-class meal for a dog, but the prince was not inclined to try them.

However, the White Dog ordered the hands to serve the Prince the dishes he liked most, and immediately, without him even mentioning his favorite food, he was provided with all the treats he could desire.

After the Prince had fulfilled his hunger, he realized that the Dog wore a bracelet on her paw, on which was a miniature of herself; but when he asked her about it, she sighed and looked so sad that, like a well-behaved prince, he said nothing more about it.

Right after supper, the hands guided him to bed. He immediately fell asleep and didn't wake up until the end of the next morning. Looking out the window, he saw that the White Dog and her companions were about to start a hunting expedition.

As soon as the hands dressed him in a green hunting suit, he ran down to join his hostess.

The hands led him to a wooden horse and seemed to be waiting for him to ride. At first, the Prince tended to be angry, but the White Dog told him with such kindness that she had no better horse to offer him, that he immediately rode, feeling very ashamed of his bad mood.

They had an excellent day of sports. The White Dog, who was riding a monkey, proved to be an intelligent hunter, ascending the highest trees with the greatest ease and without ever falling from her steed.

There has never been a more pleasant hunt, and day after day, time passed so happily that the prince completely forgot about the horse he was looking for and even forgot about his own home and his father's promise.

Finally, the White Dog reminded him that in three days, he was due to perform at court, and the Prince was awfully upset to think that he now had no chance of winning his father's kingdom. But the White Dog told him that everything would be fine and, giving him an acorn, ordered him to get on the wooden horse and leave.

The prince thought she must have been mocking him, but when she held the nut to his ear, he clearly heard a horse bark.

"Inside this acorn," she said, "is the most beautiful horse in the world. But make sure you don't open the fruit until you're in the King's presence."

The prince thanked her and, after saying goodbye to her with regret, mounted his wooden steed and left.

Before arriving at the castle, he met his two brothers, who mocked the wooden horse and also the big, ugly dog that trotted beside him.

They imagined that this was what their brother had brought in from his travels, hoping to win the prize.

When they arrived at the palace, everyone praised the two adorable horses that the older brothers brought with them, but when the youngest opened the acorn and showed a horse lying on a white satin pillow, they knew that this must be the most beautiful one in the world.

Nevertheless, the king did not sense inclined to give up his throne so far, so he expressed to the brothers that there was one more task that they should do: they should carry him a piece of muslin so fine that it would pass through the eye of a needle.

So, once again, the brothers set out on a journey. As for the newest, he mounted his wooden horse and rode back to his beloved White Dog.

She was delighted to receive him, so when the prince told her that the king had now well-ordered him to find a piece of muslin thin enough to pass through the eye of a needle, she smiled at him sweetly and told him to be in a good mood.

"In my palace, I have some very smart spinners," she said, "and I'm going to put them to work on the muslin."

The Prince had already begun to suspect that the White Dog was not just an ordinary dog, but whenever he begged her to tell him her story, she just shook her head ruefully and sighed.

Well, the second year passed as fast as the first, and the night before the day when the three princes were expected at his father's court, the White Dog gave the young Prince a nut, telling him that it contained the muslin. Then she said goodbye to him, and he got on the wooden horse and left.

Meanwhile, the young prince was so late that his brothers had already started showing their muslin pieces to the king when he arrived at the castle gates. The materials they brought were extremely fine in texture and easily passed through the hole of a darning needle, but through the small needle that the king had provided, they would not pass. Then the younger prince entered the great hall and took out his nut. He carefully broke it and found it inside a hazelnut. This, when cracked, contained a cherry; inside the cherry was a grain of wheat and in the wheat a millet seed. The Prince himself began to distrust the White Dog, but immediately felt the claw of a dog gently scratching it, so he persevered.

But the ancient king was still very unwilling to give up governing, so he told the princes that before any of them could become king, he must find a princess to marry him who was kind enough to bestow his high position; and any of the princes who carried home the gorgeous bride should really have the kingdom for themselves.

Obviously, the Prince went back to the White Dog and told her how his father behaved very unfairly to him. She consoled him as best she could and told him not to be scared, as she would introduce him to the most beautiful princess over whom the sun had already shone.

The appointed time passed happily, and one night the White Dog reminded the Prince that the next day he should return home.

"Woe is me!" he said, "Where should I find a princess now? Time is so short that I can't even look for one."

Then the White Dog told him that if he did what she asked, everything would be fine.

"Take your blade, cut off my head and tail and throw them into the flames," she said.

The prince declared that under no circumstances would he treat her so cruelly, but she begged so fervently to do what she asked that he finally consented.

As soon as he threw his head and tail into the fire, a beautiful princess appeared where the dog's body was. The spell that had been cast on her was broken, and at the same time, her courtiers and attendants, who had also turned into dogs, hurried in their proper ways again, to pay their respects to the mistress.

The prince immediately fell in love with the charming princess and begged her to accompany him to his father's court as a bride. She consented, and together they left. During the trip, the princess told her husband the story of her enchantment.

She had been raised by the elves, who treated her with great gentleness until she offended them by falling in love with a young man whose portrait the prince had seen on his paw and who looked exactly like him. Now, the fairies wanted her to marry the King of the Dwarves and were so irritated when she declared that she would not marry anyone other than her true love, that they turned her into a White Dog as punishment.

When the prince and his bride arrived at the court, everyone recognized that the princess was, by far, the most adorable lady they had ever seen. Therefore, the poor old king felt that he would now be forced to give up his kingdom. But the princess knelt beside him, kissed his hand gently, and told him that there was no reason for him to stop ruling, as she was rich enough to give each of her eldest sons a powerful kingdom, and she still had three left for herself and her dear husband. Therefore, everyone was satisfied, and there was great joy and celebration in the king's palace, and everyone lived happily ever after.

Conclusion

It will become a normal part of your life to fall asleep easily and wake up seven to eight hours later with all the energy you could ever need. All of us could use more energy, and getting into this habit will ensure you feel invigorated every time you awake.

Beyond some of the visualization strategies we explore in this guidebook, you will find there are other fantastic stories inside. Such stories are intended to help you calm your child and get them to sleep for the night, even though they're excited from daytime or have trouble calming down, and they have the values and teachings that your child needs to help with their growth. It is a perfect opportunity for you and your child to bond together to build special moments together, while in the end, always being so beneficial for your child.

CPSIA information can be obtained
at www.ICGtesting.com
Printed in the USA
BVHW061931150621
609630BV00003B/627

9 781914 533075